Richard Edwards was born in Tonbridge, Kent, and studied English and American literature at Warwick University. Since then he has lived in Italy, France and Spain. The author of some 20 picture books and books of poetry for children, his most recent titles include *Amazing Animal Alphabet* and *Nonsense Nursery Rhymes* (OUP); *Moon Frog* and *Moles Can Dance* (Walker); *You're Safe Now, Waterdog* (Orion); and *Ten Tall Oaktrees* (Red Fox). Richard Edwards lives in Edinburgh.

Susan Winter was born in South Africa and graduated from Natal University, before becoming a social worker, first in South Africa and later in London. After the birth of her second child, she studied illustration at Chelsea School of Art and began a new career as a freelance illustrator of children's books. Her previous books include *Henry's Baby* and *The Bear That Went to Ballet* (DK); the Winchelsea Trilogy and *The Ghost Watchers* (Hodder and Stoughton); *Nicky and the Twins* (Harper Collins); and *Calling All Toddlers* (Orion). Susan Winter lives in West London.

For Thomas and Max with love - *S.W.*

First published in Great Britain in 1999 by
Frances Lincoln Limited, 4 Torriano Mews
Torriano Avenue, London NW5 2RZ

First paperback edition published in 2000

British Library Cataloguing in Publication Data
available on request

ISBN 0-7112-1420-4 hardback
ISBN 0-7112-1460-3 paperback

Set in Hiroshige Book
Printed in Hong Kong

9 8 7 6 5 4 3 2

Copy Me, Copycub

Richard Edwards
Illustrated by Susan Winter

FRANCES LINCOLN

It was spring in the north woods,
and the bears were out exploring.
  Everything his mother did,
the cub did too.

When his mother splashed through a swamp,
the cub splashed through a swamp.
When his mother sat down for a scratch,
the cub sat down for a scratch.

"You know what you are," said the mother bear.
"You're a little Copycub."

From spring into summer the bears wandered, looking for good things to eat.

When his mother picked berries, Copycub picked berries.

When his mother climbed a tree for honey, Copycub climbed a tree for honey.

"Yes, you're my own little Copycub," his mother said, giving him a hug.

Autumn came, and the days grew colder. One morning when the bears awoke, there was frost on the ground.

"It's time for us to go to our cave," said the mother bear. "Winter's coming, and soon it'll be too cold to stay outside. The bearcave will shelter us from the snow. Follow me, Copycub, and keep close behind."

His mother lolloped through the trees.
Copycub lolloped through the trees.

His mother waded streams.
Copycub waded streams.

It was a long journey for a small bear. Copycub tried his best to keep up, but he was beginning to feel very tired when something cold and wet touched the end of his nose.

It was beginning to snow.

Snow fell quickly, snow fell thickly, blowing into Copycub's eyes so he could hardly see the way. Ice fringed his fur and his paws were numb with cold. He couldn't go one step further. All he wanted to do was lie down and sleep.

But his mother came back for him.

"You can't sleep here, or you'll freeze," she said.
"Come on, Copycub, the cave's not far.
Just a few more steps. Copy me."

His mother took a step.
Copycub took a step.
His mother took another step.
Copycub took another step...
and another...
and another, until...

"We're here, Copycub!"
    In a tumble of rocks was
the entrance to the bearcave.

Soon they were inside.

The cave was quiet and dry, and carpeted with leaves.

Copycub's mother hugged him until he was warm.

"We're safe now," she said. "Soon we'll be sleeping tight, and when we wake up it'll be sunny spring again."

They watched the snow falling outside. Then they snuggled down
into the leaves.

His mother yawned.
Copycub yawned.
His mother put her arms
round Copycub.
Copycub put his arms
round his mother.
His mother said,
"Good night, see you in
the springtime."
But Copycub didn't answer.

He was already asleep.

OTHER PICTURE BOOKS IN PAPERBACK FROM FRANCES LINCOLN

Arctic Song

Miriam Moss
Illustrated by Adrienne Kennaway

In the cold lands of the Arctic, a mother polar bear and her cubs break out of their winter den,
to hear an inky raven tell tales of the magic of whalesong. The cubs ask, "Where can we hear whalesong?"
They roam over land, and dive deep into an underwater world, on a poetic journey of discovery.

Suitable for National Curriculum English – Reading, Key Stages 1 and 2; Science, Key Stage 1
Scottish Guidelines English Language – Reading, Level B; Environmental Studies, Levels A and B

ISBN 0-7112-1305-4

The Time of the Lion

Caroline Pitcher
Illustrated by Jackie Morris

When Joseph sees a lion racing towards him, its great head streaming with gold, a special friendship begins.
He visits the lion's grassy den to talk, and watch the cubs at play. But one day traders come
looking for lion cubs, and Joseph suspects that his father has betrayed his newfound friends...

Suitable for National Curriculum English – Reading, Key Stages 1 and 2
Scottish Guidelines English Language – Reading, Level C

ISBN 0-7112-1338-0

Tom's Rabbit

Meredith Hooper
Illustrated by Bert Kitchen

It's very cold in Antarctica, and the *Terra Nova* is crowded with animals and men.
Tom the Sailor is looking for a quiet, cosy place for his pet rabbit. High in the rigging, down in the hold – where can
Little Rabbit make her nest? A true story of Scott's second voyage to Antarctica.

Suitable for National Curriculum English – Reading, Key Stage 1; History, Key Stage 1 and Geography, Key Stage 1
Scottish Guidelines English Language – Reading, Levels A and B; Environmental Studies, Levels A and B

ISBN 0-7112-1184-1

Frances Lincoln titles are available from all good bookshops.